D0606853

FROM APPLE TREES TO CIDER, PLEASE!

Hello!

FELICIA SANZARI CHERNESKY

PICTURES BY JULIA PATTON

ALBERT WHITMAN & COMPANY
CHICAGO, ILLINOIS

FOR THE APPLES OF MY EYE:
JESS, DAVE, JEFF, TOBY—AND EDDIE SPAGHETTI—FSC

TO MY MUMMY & DADDY, THANK YOU FOR EVERYTHING—JP

Library of Congress Cataloging-in-Publication
data is on file with the publisher.

Text copyright © 2015 Felicia Sanzari Chernesky
Pictures copyright © 2015 Albert Whitman & Company
Pictures by Julia Patton
Published in 2015 by Albert Whitman & Company
ISBN 978-0-8075-6513-1

Printed in China
10 9 8 7 6 5 4 3 2 1 HH 20 19 18 17 16 15

Design by Jordan Kost

For more information about Albert Whitman & Company,
visit our web site at www.albertwhitman.com.

Hello, apples in the trees,
growing just for Mom and me.

CIDER MILL

HOT AND COLD APPLE CIDER

PETTING ZOO

DOUGHNUTS

PUMPKIN PATCH

ENTRANCE

APPLES

Reaching up, we take our pick.
Twist and pluck them. That's the trick.

HONEYCRISP

GRANNY SMITH

Wow! Our wagon's apple full.
Mom, let's roll! I'll help you pull…

...past dappled leaves and through the loud
and happy apple-picking crowd.

Scarecrows, mums, and bales of hay
help to lead us on our way.

Here's the mill. Now let me guess.
That's an apple cider press!

OFF→
←ON

U-
PICK

Clean the apples. Check for worms.

Wash and dry them. No more germs.

Every apple does its part,
whether juicy sweet or tart.

PULL
TO
STOP

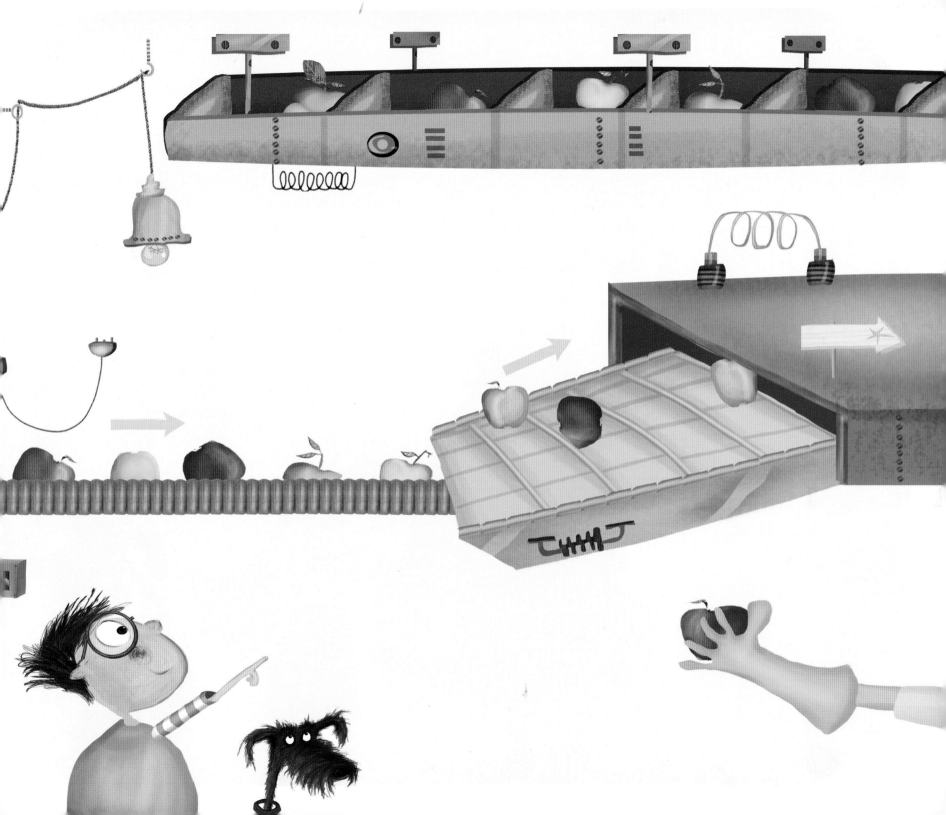

Red, green, yellow—drop them in!
Turn the crank. The shredder spins.

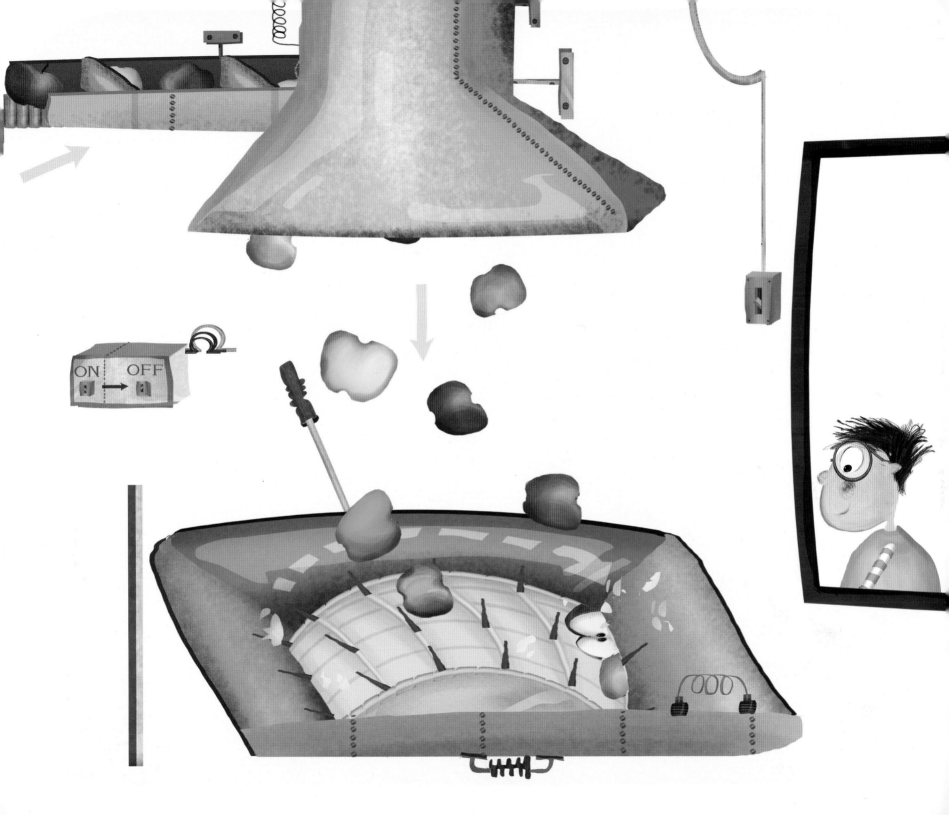

Wind the metal wheel to crush.

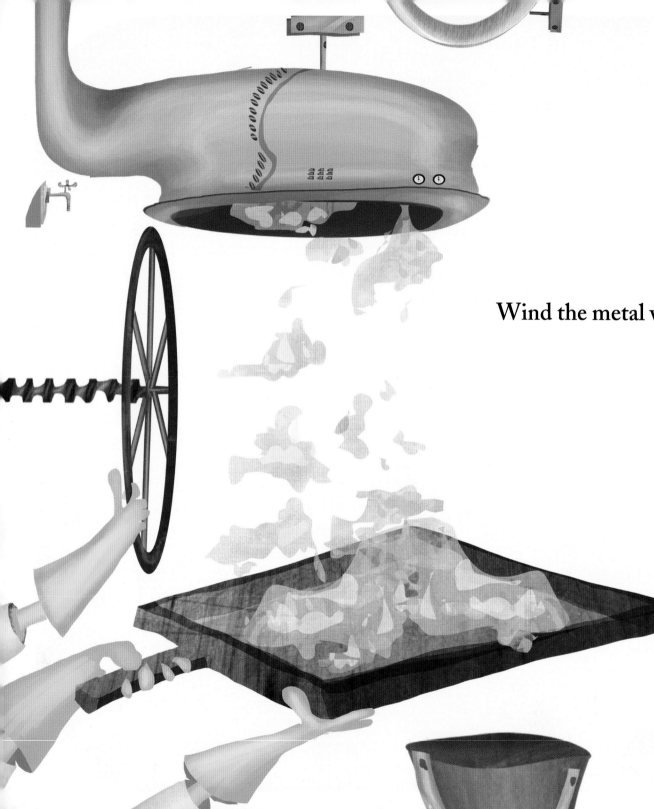

In the bucket: apple mush.

Twist and press to squish and mash.

See the cider splish and splash!

Turn the tap to fill the jug.
Hear the cider, *glug, glug, glug.*

Mom, I'm thirsty. Can we stay? There's a festival today!

CIDER MILL

PUMPKIN PATCH

APPLE MUFFINS and PIES

HOT 'N' COLD CIDER

TOFFEE candy.APPLES

APPLES

apple cider

Come and get it! Gather near.
Gobble up some apple cheer.

Cobbler, fritters, pie, the rest…

I like cider doughnuts best.

Gulp it cold or sip it hot—
apple cider hits the spot!

Apple smiles. So glad we stayed.
Now we know how cider's made!